The BUNNY BOOK

By Patsy Scarry • Illustrated by Richard Scarry

A GOLDEN BOOK • NEW YORK

Copyright © 1955, renewed 1983 by Random House, Inc. All rights reserved under International and Pan-American Copyright Conventions. Published in the United States by Golden Books, an imprint of Random House Children's Books, a division of Random House, Inc., New York, and simultaneously in Canada by Random House of Canada Limited, Toronto. Originally published in 1955 by Simon and Schuster, Inc., and Artists and Writers Guild, Inc. Golden Books, A Golden Book, A Little Golden Book, the G colophon, and the distinctive gold spine are registered trademarks of Random House, Inc. A Little Golden Book Classic is a trademark of Random House, Inc.
Library of Congress Control Number: 2004103054
ISBN 0-375-83224-6
www.goldenbooks.com
Printed in the United States of America
First Random House Edition 2005
20 19 18 17 16 15 14 13 12 11

FOR HUCK

THE DADDY BUNNY tossed his baby in the air.

"What will our baby be when he grows up?" asked the daddy bunny.

"He will be a policeman with gold buttons on his suit,"
said the mother bunny. "He will help little lost children
find their mothers and daddies."

"Maybe he will be a circus clown," said the daddy bunny. "He will wear a funny suit and do funny tricks to make the children laugh."

"Why can't our baby be a cowboy?" asked the bunny brother. "If he grows up to be a cowboy he can ride horses at the rodeo."

But the baby bunny did not want to be a policeman or a circus clown or a cowboy when he grew up.

He sat in his basket and smiled at his bunny family. He knew what he would be.

"I think our baby bunny should be an airplane pilot,"
said the little bunny sister. "He could fly into the sky.
And when he felt like having fun he could jump out in
his parachute."

"Maybe he will be a fireman," said his Great Aunt Bunny. "Then he could drive a big ladder truck to all the fires. He would be a brave fireman."

Great Uncle Bunny wanted the baby to be an engineer on a big train.

"He would ring the bell when he was ready to start the train. And blow his horn, Toot! Toot! in the tunnels," said Great Uncle Bunny.

But the baby bunny did not want to be an airplane pilot or a fireman or an engineer on a big train when he grew up. He nibbled on his carrot and looked wise. He knew what he wanted to be.

Old Grandaddy Bunny said:
"Just look at that baby. Why, any bunny can see he is
going to be a lion tamer!"

But Grandma Bunny said:
"I think he will be a nice little mailman who will bring a
letter to every house and make the neighbors happy."

A hungry little bunny cousin wished that the baby would have a candy store.

"He could make lollypops with funny faces and give them to all the good children," wished the hungry little bunny cousin.

But the baby bunny did not want to be a
lion tamer or a mailman or have a candy store.
He shook his rattle and smiled.
He would be what he wanted to be.

The little girl cousin said:
"It would be nice if our baby was a doctor. Then he
could put big bandages on little bumps."

"Oh dear no," said Aunt Bunny. "I am sure he will be a
lifeguard at the beach. He will save people who can't swim."

"Not at all, my dear," said Uncle Bunny. "This little baby may grow up to be a farmer with a fine red tractor."

But the baby bunny did not want to be a doctor or a
lifeguard or a farmer with a fine red tractor when he grew up.
He bounced on his daddy's knee and laughed.
Can you guess what he will be?

The baby bunny will be a daddy rabbit!
That is what he will be—with lots of little bunny
children to feed when they are hungry.

He will be a nice daddy who will chase the children
when they want to be chased.

And give them presents on their birthdays.

He will read them a story when they are sleepy.

And tuck them into bed at night.
And that is what the baby bunny will grow up to be.
A daddy rabbit.